*When the Joker captures the Commissioner
of Police, Batman goes to the rescue. But the
Joker has laid many traps along the way...
he is out to get the Caped Crusader.*

British Library Cataloguing in Publication Data

Hatch, Constance V.
    Funhouse of fear.
    I. Title   II. Howarth, Walter   III. Series
    813'.54 [F]
    ISBN 0-7214-1235-1

First edition

Published by Ladybird Books Ltd Loughborough Leicestershire UK
Ladybird Books Inc Auburn Maine 04210 USA
Printed in England

BAT MAN
FUNHOUSE OF FEAR

by Constance V Hatch
illustrated by Walter Howarth

Ladybird Books

The Bat-Signal split the night sky like cannonfire. Batman was needed!

The Batmobile sped through the streets of Gotham City. When he arrived at police headquarters, Batman found no sign of Commissioner Gordon. Instead, he was greeted by the Chief of Police.

"Where's the Commissioner?" asked Batman.

"That's the trouble. He's disappeared," said the Chief. "An hour ago, we received this." He handed a small pink card to Batman. It read, "He who laughs last, laughs loudest!"

"What do you suppose it means, Batman?" asked the Chief.

"It's the sort of card dispensed from fortune-telling machines, the kind found in amusement parks," said Batman, after examining the card.

"But the only one of those for miles around is Gotham Amusement Park. And that's closed for the season!" objected the Chief.

"That would only make it easier for some crafty villain to use it as a hide-out... and it's probably the Joker! The idea of using an amusement park as a base would appeal to him and so would this message about 'who laughs last!'"

"So you think he's kidnapped the Commissioner?" asked the Police Chief.

"Yes! There's no time to lose!" said Batman.

Faster than thought, the Batmobile pulled up outside the Gotham Amusement Park. The front gate had been altered to look like the grinning face of the Joker himself.

Batman stood still and looked carefully around him. Everything had been boarded up for the winter. Every ride was still. Only the cars of the big wheel creaked eerily in the wind. There was no sign of life, except for the faint, tinny sound of a fairground organ wafting on the breeze.

Batman followed the sound of the music. It grew louder and louder until he found its source.

KEEP OUT
BY ORDER

It was the funhouse, as brightly lit up as when the amusement park was open. The lights blinked invitingly as the music grew louder.

The Caped Crusader entered cautiously. "This is the Joker's idea of a challenge," he thought. "He's laid some carefully prepared trap, but I'm going to have to go in... to find Commissioner Gordon!"

Batman found himself in a small white corridor that seemed to grow narrower the farther he went. He suddenly realised that the corridor was growing smaller because the walls were closing in.

All at once, grey, glinting knives sprang from the walls, threatening to tear him to shreds. Closer and closer came the knives, and closer and closer came the walls, until at last Batman was fighting to hold them apart at arm's length.

Suddenly, his arm brushed against one of the menacing blades. It bent! It sprang back into shape with a bounce! The knives were made of rubber!

Then, when Batman grabbed one of the knives for support, it swung downwards with a clunk. It was really a secret lever, operating a trapdoor!

As the floor gave way, the crimefighter heard the Joker's ringing laugh. But Batman was always ready for anything and he landed on his feet. Staring through the inky blackness, he thought he saw a flash of white teeth and moved forward carefully, hoping to trap the Joker in the dark.

Suddenly the lights came on, and there stood an angry, fierce gorilla dressed in a

clown suit. "Kong-gratulations, Batman!" boomed the Joker's voice from a hidden speaker. "For what my little pet will do to you... you have my chimp-pathy! Ha ha!"

The gorilla lunged, and only Batman's speed saved him. He took a small tranquilliser dart gun from his belt and fired it at the huge beast. Within seconds, the gorilla was snoring like a baby – lying in front of the only door in the room.

Batman pulled the gorilla out of the way and opened the door to find a staircase, with the Joker nearly at the top. He chased the Joker as far up as he could, but the villain had quickly opened the door at the top and slammed it behind him, locking Batman out.

The Caped Crusader opened the door with his lockpick to find yet another darkened room. But this time, when the lights came on, Batman saw nothing but bars where the walls should be. He was in a cage – and the floor was moving.

Gears hummed as the cage went down like a lift – into an immense tank of water. Batman was going to drown!

He didn't have much time. He pulled a laser saw from his belt, and cut a hole through the bars. As he escaped from the cage, he gripped his underwater torch to help him to see.

He swam around under the cage, looking for a way out, but there was no exit there. There *was* however a giant squid. Already it was uncoiling its tentacles, its eyes on Batman. If it caught him in its grip, Batman was done for!

He took rapid evasive action but the squid
kept coming closer! Batman took an ordinary
fountain pen from his belt and squirted ink in
the squid's face, using its own kind of
defence against it. Blinded, the squid
stopped in its tracks.

By now, the water had buoyed Batman up
higher and higher. He reached the surface
and saw above him an open doorway. The
Joker appeared there, making faces at him.
"You'll never catch me!" he sneered.

When the Joker vanished, Batman pulled out a hook with a rope attached to it and fired it to land just above the centre of the doorway. Then he climbed up the rope out of the water and walked into the new entrance.

Batman was surprised to see – the Joker! It was a reflection in a giant mirror. As he walked, he saw hundreds of mirrors, all casting the Joker's reflection at him. "Welcome to my Hall of Mirrors!" said the Joker's voice from nowhere. "Don't believe all you see!"

Then the Joker's reflections disappeared, to be replaced by hundreds of reflections of Police Commissioner Gordon. The Commissioner was tied to a chair, with a ri of small flames round him. Directly over h' head was a small sprinkler.

The Joker's voice boomed, "Looking for
meone? Since you can't find the real me,
trick here is to find the real Commissioner
don! By the way, I've set the floor around
n fire! You'd better rescue him in time!"

As the flames grew higher, Batman heard the Joker's voice again. "But I'm being a sport about this! Look behind you!" The spotlight hit a carnival test-your-strength game, with a huge bell at the top. A huge mallet stood next to it. "If you can use all your strength to ring the bell at the top, it will automatically set off the sprinkler. Who says I don't play fair? And for now... goodbye!"

500

450

400

350

300

The Joker play fair? What a hope! When Batman picked up the mallet, he discovered it was made of foam rubber! There was no way he could strike the game and ring the gong with it!

There was only one thing to do. He leapt onto the machine with a tremendous jump. His strength was so great that the ringing bell at the top flew right off.

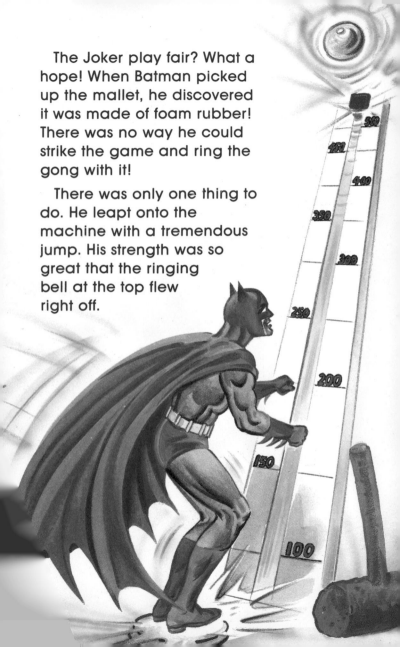

All at once, the sprinkler came on, dousing the flames... and the Commissioner! Batman snapped a Batarang from his utility belt and threw it at one mirror, shattering it completely. It ricocheted off and bounced to the next mirror, reducing it to splinters as well. The Batarang leapt from mirror to mirror, smashing each one, in a hailstorm of broken glass.

Finally, only the real Commissioner
remained. Batman cut his bonds with a knife,
and they darted to the funhouse exit. It had
been altered to look like the Joker's grinning
face just as the entrance had. The teeth of
the Joker's smile were opening and closing
rapidly. "Jump when I say!" commanded
Batman, and on his signal, they leapt
through the chattering teeth. They made it!

Gordon thanked Batman and said, "The Joker's probably far from here by now! Who knows where he'll strike next?"

"I don't think he's gone far at all," said Batman. "I didn't see anything he could escape in when I surveyed the area on my arrival." But as he spoke, a beeper sounded. "That's the Batmobile! The Joker's trying to steal it to get away!"

They ran to the side of Batman's amazing car just in time to see the Joker slam the door. But the car wouldn't start. And when the Joker tried to get out again he had no luck at all.

"My Batmobile becomes a prison to anyone who tries to enter and steal it," Batman told the Commissioner.

Soon the police arrived to take the Joker into custody. Two tough sergeants led him away in handcuffs. "I'll get you some day," growled the villain, looking back.

Batman grinned. "Maybe we'll meet again, but for now, *I'm* having the last laugh!"